Cat Power!

Daniel Kirk

Hyperion Books for Children
New York

First Edition
1 3 5 7 9 10 8 6 4 2
ISBN-13: 978-1-4231-0081-2
ISBN-10: 1-4231-0081-6

Library of Congress Cataloging-in-Publication Data on file.
Printed in Singapore
Reinforced binding

Visit www.hyperionbooksforchildren.com

Table of Contents

CAT POWER!

I was adored in ancient Egypt,
I was revered in classic Rome.
Four thousand years of wandering
have brought me to your home!
Phoenician traders sailing ships
spread my kind far and near.
Humans bade me welcome,
but cat power brought me here.

Felida, *gato*, *qitah*, *neko*,
the world's my habitat.
Humans name me many things,
but you may call me *cat*!
I'll be the master of the house,
while I'm your honored guest.
My sweet face gets me in the door;
cat power does the rest.

Confucius once kept kin of mine,
Muhammad owned cats, too.
Kings and sultans sing my praises,
I'm regal through and through.
In your own country, forty million
cat fans can't be wrong;
my beauty makes me special . . .
cat power makes me strong.

Yes, I'm proud and elegant;
it's true what others say.
Graceful, treasured, pampered,
that's the role I'm born to play!
My habits make me charming,
my independence makes me free.
You made me your favorite pet—
cat power makes me *me*!

Symphony

Still as a statue,
in shadows I lie.
To the top of the tree,
all the little birds fly.

First comes a chirp,
then it's joined by a cheep.
The symphony's started
as closer I creep.

6

They twitter, they warble,
they whistle, they sing.
The music birds make
is a wonderful thing.

I leap for the tree trunk
with joy in my eyes.
The birds flutter skyward,
and shriek in surprise.

"Your music is wonderful,
come back!" I call,
but not one returns;
I'm a cat, after all!

butterflies

More delicate than bumblebees,
adrift on whispers of a breeze,
from heaven-heights they gently float
like sails on a windblown boat.

Across a dome of sky so vast,
like flags that flutter from a mast,
flapping gently, airborne, free,
they sweep in silent dignity.

They light awhile, and then depart,
and touch each blossom's perfumed heart.
Their wings are painted daintily,
in rainbow colors cats can't see!

My paw springs up, my claws a rake,
but swiping just for swiping's sake;
my hunting skills, as sharp as nails,
I'll save for crickets, ants, and snails,

and bugs less pleasing to the eye.
I'd never eat a butterfly!
Here in the garden, I am blessed
to treasure things that I love best:

the friendly call of buzzing bees,
the tiny tickle of a breeze,
the warm embrace of sun-blue skies,
and insect angels—butterflies!

You say I'm looking sickly, so,
it's to the vet that I must go.
Don't take me from my home, oh please,
just because I cough and sneeze.
If that's your plan, I'll cry and cling.
Don't put me in that cat-cage thing!

Don't make me beg, don't make me plead.
A vet's the one thing I don't need!
Don't start the car and put me in it,
I'm getting better by the minute!
Don't drive so fast, no need to hurry—
for I am only sick with worry.

I am not ill, I swear I'm not.
Don't let that vet give me a shot!
Don't drag me screaming to my doom,
save me from the waiting room—
All those desperate, frightened pets
who can't stand visits to their vets!

The haunted stares, the smell of fear—
I don't know what I'm doing here!
I'm all choked up—alas, alack!
HACK HACK HACK HACK HACK HACK HACK!
Hey, look, there's nothing wrong with me.
I just coughed up a hair ball,
see?

THE VET

11

alley cat

Moonlight meandering,
I make plans
down fire escapes,
past garbage cans.
Got no time for idle chat.
Make way—I'm an alley cat!

I'm a lean, mean, hungry beast . . .
soon on trash-bag treats I'll feast—
fish heads, scraps,
and alley mice.
Don't care if you think I'm nice!

Wanna fight me?
Wanna bite me?
Wanna kick, and claw,
and scratch?
If you've the muscle for a tussle,
I will meet you in a match.

Full-moon fever
stalks my brain;
got no fear
and feel no pain.
Howling, yowling for a spat—
don't mess with an alley cat!

Panic strikes.
My senses spin.
No longer can I hold it in.
My tail tucked low, my ears aquiver,
beside the bathroom door I shiver
from my whiskers to my socks.
Behold—
the dreaded litter box!

Things are buried there,
I know,
that I expelled
two weeks ago . . .
and I am not
the kind of critter
to set my paws
in soiled litter.

I may be forced to void my bowels
on carpets, easy chairs, or towels. . . .
Perhaps I'll be inclined, instead,
to do my business
on your bed!
I will not use that box—
I MEAN IT!
Won't someone kindly come and clean it?

litter box

PRETEND

It's a snake in the grass,
it's a sewer rat's tail,
it's a fishing line hooked
on the lip of a whale.
It's a length of unraveling
string on a kite.
It's a quick-burning fuse
on some live dynamite.

It's a long lion whisker,
a strong leather whip,
it's the anchor line tied
to the bow of a ship.
It's a strand of a spiderweb,
sticky and taut.
It's an octopus tentacle—
help me, I'm caught!

It's the leash on a bulldog,
the reins of a horse—
but it's all just a game
I am playing, of course.
It's only pretend,
it's a make-believe thing . . .
I have lots of fun
with a big ball of string!

Hunter

I am a hunter;
my senses are keen.
Rats find me frightening,
birds say I am mean.
I'm sharp-eyed, lightning-clawed,
wealthy in stealth—
mice declare I'm no good for their health.
To wait by the bushes,
to stake out a nest,
to hunt is my nature—
it's what I do best!
It's my purpose, my fate, my joy, and my habit
to sneak up on my prey—
and then
simply
NAB IT!

19

Treetop Tom

I shadowed a squirrel through the neighbor's backyard;
he shot up this sycamore tree.
When I'd climbed to the top, the squirrel scurried back down;
now there's nobody up here but me!
I guess I'll just rest and admire the view.
From this branch, I can see the whole town.
It isn't so hard climbing up to the top—
but I
really
can't
stand
going
down!

Rub-a-Rub-Rub

Rub-a-rub-rub,
it's time for my grub,
so I'm rubbing my fur on your leg.
I'm purring,
and pushing . . .
Come on with that can!
Get it open,
and don't make me beg!

Rub-a-rub-rub,
make it snappy, there, bub,
I'm pressing my pelt
on your shin.
If I push any harder,
I'll knock us both over.
Come on, scrape the chow
from that tin!

Rub-a-rub-rub,
after all that hubbub,
what's that slop that you plopped
in my dish?
If you think I'll try liver,
then keep thinking, mister—
you know I eat
nothing but fish!

22

the gift

When I think of you, I feel thankful and glad.
You're the very best owner a cat's ever had.
You serve me the finest meals three times a day,
you go fetch a yarn ball when I want to play.
But yet, as a cat (it's sad, but it's true),
I know I take more than I give to you.

And so I decided, since I'm in your debt,
to give you a present you'll never forget.
I gave it some thought, and then, certain and swift,
I knew what would be the appropriate gift.
You don't have to thank me—no, don't say a word. . . .
To show that I care,
here's a pretty, dead bird!

THE

Everyone loves me, it's true!
The judges all say "Aaah!" and "Oooh!"
Now, between you and me,
it's quite easy to see
all the ribbons I win will be blue!

CONTEST

There sits the cat I despise,
a triumphant look in her eyes;
she's the one they adore,
with the most perfect score;
don't they know I deserve the first prize?

Prancing, Leaping
Dancing, Sleeping
Stretching, Stalking
Grooming, Walking
Crouching, Yowling
Prowling cat—
    my bliss is without measure.

Climbing, Running
Resting, Sunning
Sitting, Pouncing
Twisting, Bouncing
Snatching, Pacing
Racing cat—
    the whole world is my treasure.

CAT!

Spitting, Hissing
Flitting, Kissing
Rubbing, Sneaking
Scratching, Peeking
Purring, Scheming
Dreaming cat—
    yes, I was born for pleasure!

Cat on a Leash

Nowhere to run,
no place to hide,
I'm shamed, embarrassed, mortified.
Can't dash away,
can't climb a tree,
because you put a leash on me.
Because you feel that you must walk me,
all the world will surely mock me,
flock to me,
gawk at me,
laugh at me—
sheesh!
A cat's not meant to wear a leash!

Scritch,
scratch,
scratch,
scritch,
got a yearning,
got an itch.
Got to do what I love most,
work on my old scratching post.

Tug and tear,
pull and scrape,
keep my claws
in ripping shape—
razor sharp,
tough as steel,
get the perfect
paw appeal.

That carpet-covered tube is toast . . .
I'll work on my old scratching post.
Do it harder,
do it fast,
scratch,
scritch,
scritch,
scratch.

scratching post

I WANT TO GO OUT!

The moon's coming up, night creeps over the land.
I prowl by the back door, so you'll understand.
I push with my paws, I pace and I pout.
Open the door, please, I want to go out!

I've got things to do, and places to go.
You really should listen, you really should know.
Do you understand what this fuss is about?
Open the door, please, I want to go out!

I'm getting annoyed now, I'm not having fun.
This night will be over before it's begun!
I'm scratching and scraping, and there is no doubt—
Open the door, please, I want to go out!

All right, now, I'm angry, I'm fuming, I'm peeved.
So much complaining, so little achieved!
I howl and I yowl, I screech and I shout—
Open the door, please, I want to go out!

Finally, freedom! You opened the door.
My crying was simply too hard to ignore.
But what's this? Good heavens, it's starting to rain.
Who, me? Going out? Do you think I'm insane?

Some would say I'm overweight;
I carry quite a pouch.
I mosey to the kitchen,
then pad back to the couch.
Ten times a day I make this trip—
I don't know what's the matter.
Despite my constant exercise,
I just keep getting fatter!

fat cat

I see you by the window,
sitting in your favorite chair.
A golden shaft of sunlight
streams in through the quiet air.
I slip across the room,
for one thing's better than a nap.
I make a little sound, and spring,
and land upon your lap.

You smile and put your book aside
so I can settle in.
I stretch and lift my head up high
so you can scratch my chin.
Something magic happens
every time you stroke my fur;
I close my eyes a tiny bit
and I begin to *purrrrrrrrrrrrrr*. . . .

A funny little rumble,
like an earthquake, grows inside,
then ripples through me, so
I couldn't stop it if I tried.
I purr because I love you,
but I can't tell you that.
I purr because I'm happy . . .
and because I am a cat!

Purrrrrrr

Dedicated to Mary Gorton,
lifelong cat fancier

Music on the CD is performed by:

Paul Byrne Studio (tracks 2, 3, 7, 9, 11, 12, 13 14, 18)
Paul Byrne: acoustic and electric guitars, mandolin,
dobro, string and horn arrangements
Daniel Kirk: vocals
Kate Brennan: vocals
Steve DeLuca: percussion
Cheryl Huerta: cello
Brett Dubner: viola

Chris Bolger Studio (tracks 1, 4, 5, 6, 8, 10, 15, 16, 17)
Chris Bolger: 4 and 12 string bass, acoustic, electric
and baritone guitars, electric sitar
Daniel Kirk: vocals, acoustic and electric guitars
Dennis Diken: drums
Charlie Potters: piano and organ
Les Elfenbein: piano
Ruth and Laura Bolger: background vocals

Recorded, produced, and mixed by Paul Byrne and Chris Bolger, 2007

Special thanks to Paul and Chris for their advice, expertise, and
commitment; Julia Gorton for creative and emotional support; and Madeline
and Frederick for their help getting Lily the cat to cooperate
for the jacket photograph and endpapers.

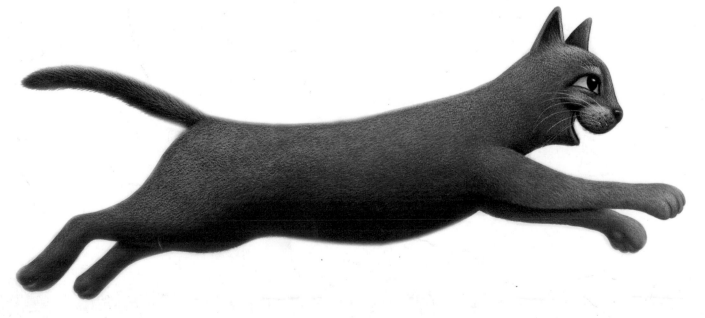